BREMEN

CHIMNEY CORNER STORIES

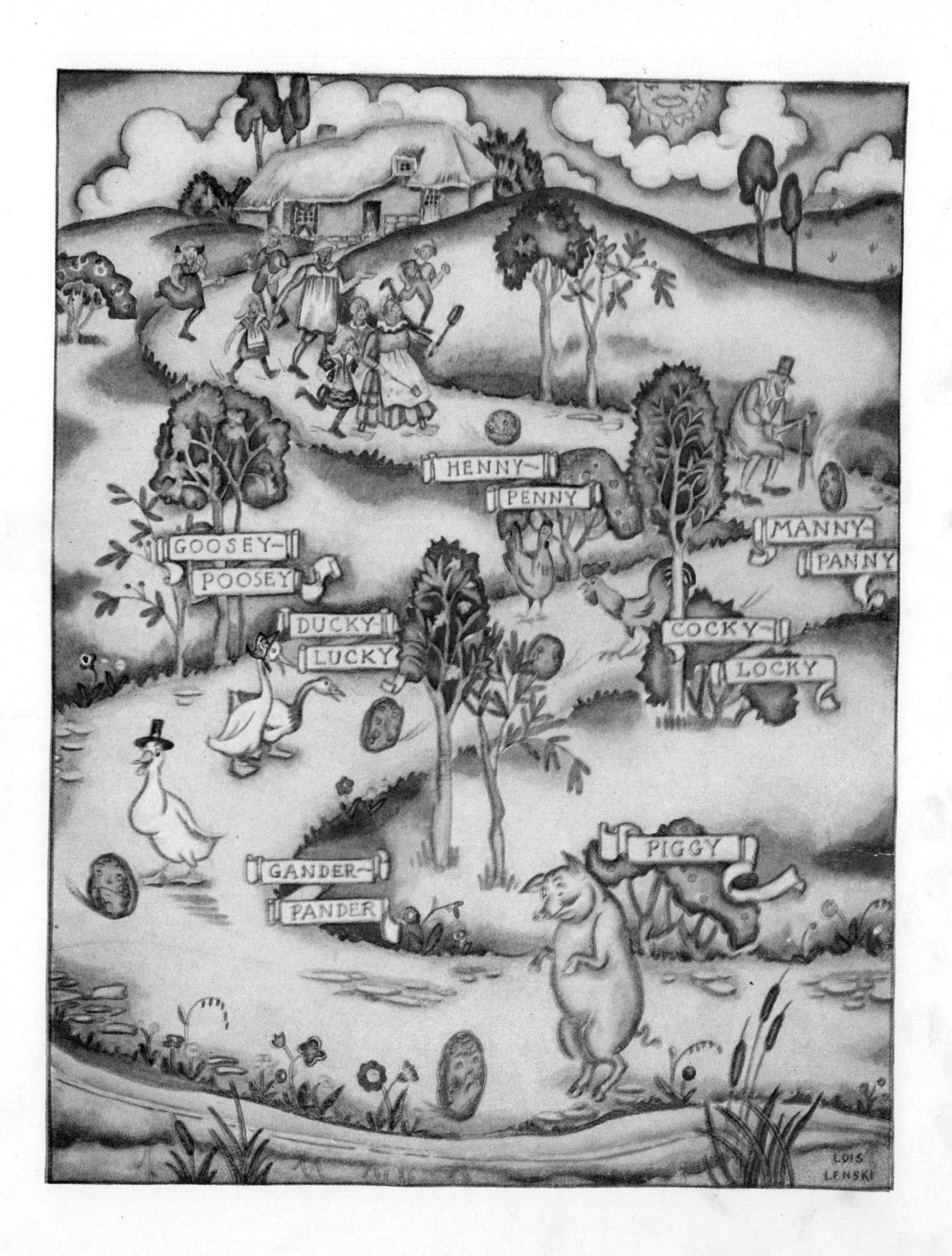
HENNY-
PENNY
MANNY-
PANNY
GOOSEY-
POOSEY
DUCKY-
LUCKY
COCKY-
LOCKY
PIGGY
GANDER-
PANDER
LOIS
LENSKI

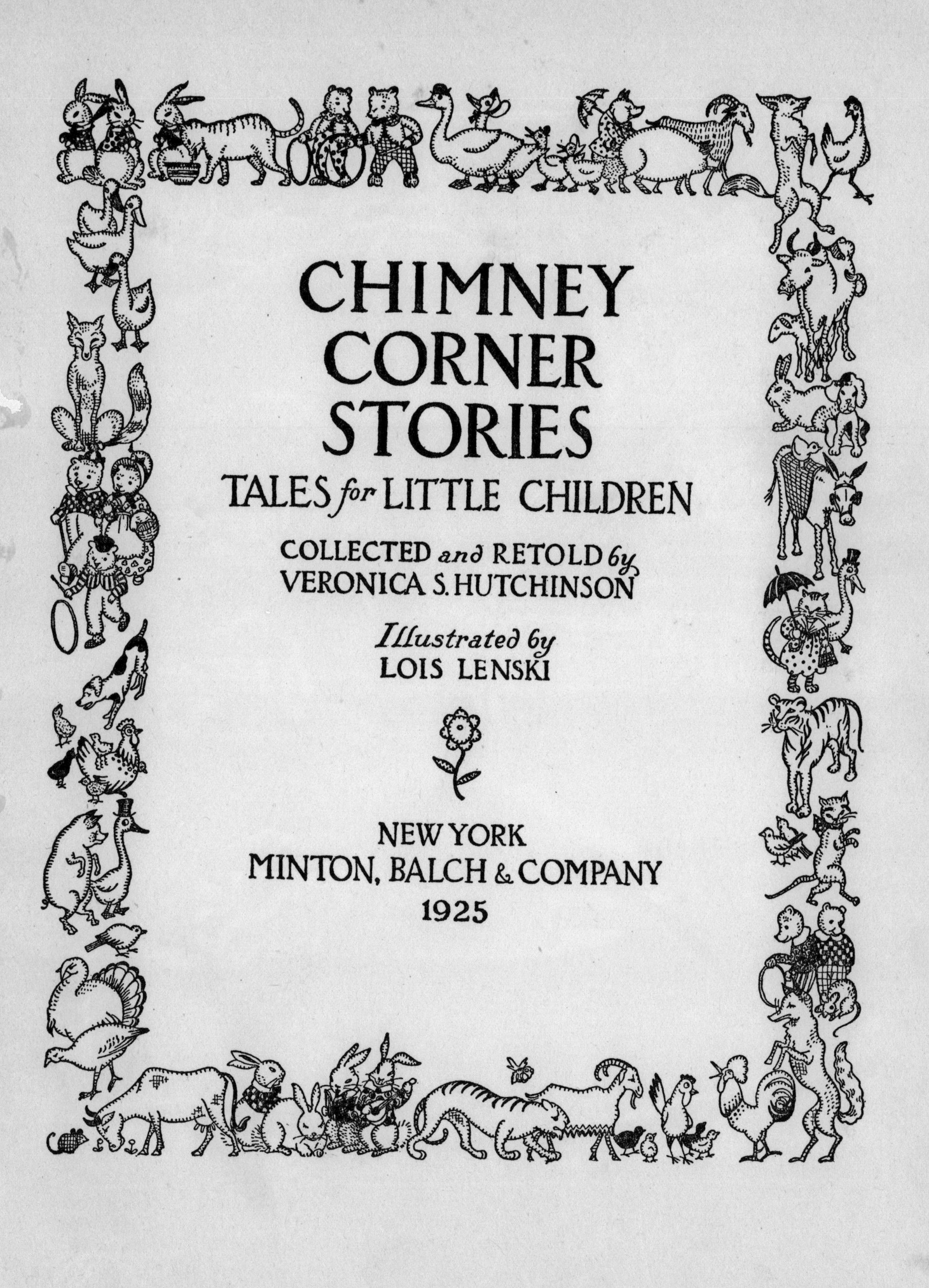

CHIMNEY CORNER STORIES

TALES *for* LITTLE CHILDREN

COLLECTED *and* RETOLD *by*
VERONICA S. HUTCHINSON

Illustrated by
LOIS LENSKI

NEW YORK
MINTON, BALCH & COMPANY
1925

Second Printing, December, 1925
Third Printing, August, 1927
Fourth Printing, July, 1929
Fifth Printing, September, 1930

Printed in the United States of America by
J. J. LITTLE & IVES COMPANY, NEW YORK

To

FOUR LITTLE GIRLS

JEAN, LORENE, ELIZABETH ANN AND PATRICIA,

and to

THREE LITTLE BOYS

JACK, HOWDY AND JOHN,

THIS BOOK IS AFFECTIONATELY DEDICATED

How am I to sing your praise,
Happy chimney-corner days,
Sitting safe in nursery nooks,
Reading picture story-books?

—From "A Child's Garden of Verses"
by Robert Louis Stevenson

CONTENTS

Henny Penny

HENNY PENNY

ONE day Henny Penny was picking up corn in the farmyard, when an acorn fell out of a tree and struck her on the head.

"Goodness gracious me!" said Henny Penny, "the sky is falling. I must go and tell the King."

So she went along and she went along and she went along until she met Cocky Locky.

"Where are you going, Henny Penny?" asked Cocky Locky.

"Oh," said Henny Penny, "the sky is falling and I am going to tell the King."

"May I go with you, Henny Penny?" asked Cocky Locky.

"Certainly," said Henny Penny.

So Henny Penny and Cocky Locky went to tell the King that the sky was falling.

They went along and they went along and they went along, until they met Ducky Daddles.

"Where are you going, Henny Penny and Cocky Locky?" asked Ducky Daddles.

"Oh, we are going to tell the King that the sky is falling," said Henny Penny and Cocky Locky.

"May I go with you?" asked Ducky Daddles.

"Certainly," said Henny Penny and Cocky Locky.

So Henny Penny, Cocky Locky, and Ducky Daddles went to tell the King that the sky was falling.

They went along and they went along and they went along until they met Goosey Poosey.

"Where are you going, Henny Penny, Cocky Locky, and Ducky Daddles?" asked Goosey Poosey.

"Oh, we are going to tell the King the sky is falling," said Henny Penny, Cocky Locky, and Ducky Daddles.

"May I go with you?" asked Goosey Poosey.

"Certainly," said Henny Penny, Cocky Locky, and Ducky Daddles.

So Henny Penny, Cocky Locky, Ducky Daddles and Goosey Poosey went to tell the King that the sky was falling.

They went along and they went along and they went along until they met Turkey Lurkey.

"Where are you going, Henny Penny, Cocky Locky, Ducky Daddles, and Goosey Poosey?" asked Turkey Lurkey.

"Oh, we are going to tell the King the sky is falling," said Henny Penny, Cocky Locky, Ducky Daddles, and Goosey Poosey.

"May I go with you?" asked Turkey Lurkey.

"Certainly," said Henny Penny, Cocky Locky, Ducky Daddles, and Goosey Poosey.

So Henny Penny, Cocky Locky, Ducky Daddles, Goosey Poosey, and Turkey Lurkey went on to tell the King the sky was falling.

They went along and they went along and they went along until they met Foxy Woxy.

"Where are you going, Henny Penny, Cocky Locky, Ducky Daddles, Goosey Poosey, and Turkey Lurkey?" asked Foxy Woxy.

"Oh, we are going to tell the King the sky is fall-

LOIS LENSKI

ing," said Henny Penny, Cocky Locky, Ducky Daddles, Goosey Poosey, and Turkey Lurkey.

"Oh, but that is not the way to the King, Henny Penny, Cocky Locky, Ducky Daddles, Goosey Poosey, and Turkey Lurkey," said Foxy Woxy, "come with me and I will show you a short way to the King's Palace."

"Certainly," said Henny Penny, Cocky Locky, Ducky Daddles, Goosey Poosey, and Turkey Lurkey.

They went along and they went along and they went along until they reached Foxy Woxy's Cave. In they went after Foxy Woxy, and they never came out again.

To this day the King has never been told that the sky was falling.

The Old Woman and her Pig

The Old WOMAN and HER PIG

ONCE upon a time an old woman was sweeping her house. She found a crooked sixpence.

"What shall I do with this sixpence?" she said to herself. "I will go to the market and buy a little pig."

So away she went and bought a little pig; but as she was coming home she came to a stile. The piggy would not go over the stile no matter how she coaxed.

She went a little farther and she met a dog. So she said, "Dog! dog! bite pig; piggy won't jump over the stile, and I shall not get home to-night."

But the dog would not.

She went a little farther and she met a stick. So she said, "Stick! stick! beat dog; dog won't bite pig; piggy won't jump over the stile; and I shall not get home to-night."

But the stick would not.

She went a little farther and she met a fire. She said, "Fire! fire! burn stick; stick won't beat dog; dog won't bite pig; piggy won't jump over the stile; and I shall not get home to-night."

But the fire would not.

She went a little farther and she met some water. So she said, "Water! water! quench fire; fire won't burn stick; stick won't beat dog; dog won't bite pig; piggy won't jump over the stile; and I shall not get home to-night."

But the water would not.

She went a little farther and she met an ox. So she said, "Ox! ox! drink water; water won't quench fire; fire won't burn stick; stick won't beat dog; dog

LOIS
LENSKI

won't bite pig; piggy won't jump over the stile; and I shall not get home to-night."

But the ox would not.

She went a little farther and she met a butcher. So she said, "Butcher! butcher! kill ox; ox won't drink water; water won't quench fire; fire won't burn stick; stick won't beat dog; dog won't bite pig; piggy won't jump over the stile; and I shall not get home to-night."

But the butcher would not.

She went a little farther and she met a rope. So she said, "Rope! rope! hang butcher; butcher won't kill ox; ox won't drink water; water won't quench fire; fire won't burn stick; stick won't beat dog; dog won't bite pig; piggy won't jump over the stile; and I shall not get home to-night."

But the rope would not.

She went a little farther and she met a rat. So she said, "Rat! rat! gnaw rope; rope won't hang butcher; butcher won't kill ox; ox won't drink water; water won't quench fire; fire won't burn stick; stick won't beat dog; dog won't bite pig; piggy won't jump over the stile; and I shall not get home to-night."

But the rat would not.

She went a little farther and she met a cat. So she said, "Cat! cat! eat rat; rat won't gnaw rope; rope won't hang butcher; butcher won't kill ox; ox won't drink water; water won't quench fire; fire won't burn stick; stick won't beat dog; dog won't bite pig; piggy won't jump over the stile; and I shall not get home to-night."

But the cat said, "If you will go to yonder cow and bring me a saucer of milk, I will kill the rat."

Away went the old woman to the cow.

The cow said, "If you will go over to that far haystack, and bring me a handful of hay, I will give you milk."

Away went the old woman to the haystack and brought the hay to the cow.

As soon as the cow had eaten the hay, she gave the old woman a saucer of milk; away she went with it to the cat.

When the cat lapped up the milk, the cat began to kill the rat, the rat began to gnaw the rope, the rope began to hang the butcher, the butcher began to kill the ox, the ox began to drink the water, the water began to quench the fire, the fire began to burn the stick, the stick began to beat the dog, the dog began to bite the pig, the little pig squealed and jumped over the stile; and the old woman went home that night.

The Pancake

THE PANCAKE

ONCE upon a time there was a mother who had seven hungry children. She was making a milk Pancake for supper. There it was, a sizzling and a frying and a sizzling and a frying, and oh, it looked so good! The seven hungry children stood around watching it, and the father sat down and looked on.

The first child said, "Oh, dear mother, give me a bite."

The second said, "Oh, dear good mother, give me a bite."

The third said, "Oh, dear sweet mother, give me a bite."

The fourth said, "Oh, dear sweet darling mother, give me a bite."

The fifth one said, "Oh, dear sweet darling best mother, give me a bite."

The sixth one said, "Oh, dear sweet darling dearest mother, give me a bite."

The seventh one said, "Oh, dear sweet darling loveliest mother, give me a bite."

"Now, children," said the mother, "just wait a moment until the Pancake turns itself." She should have said, "Now, children, wait a moment until I turn the Pancake," because as soon as she said,

"Wait until the Pancake turns itself," the Pancake heard and was so frightened it flopped over on one side and fried nice and brown, then flopped over on the other side and fried nice and brown, then jumped right out of the frying pan, rolled out of the kitchen door, down the garden walk, through the garden gate, and down the road.

The seven hungry children, the Mother, and the Father ran after it, all of them calling, "Oh, Pancake, stop a moment. We want a bite of you."

But the Pancake rolled on and on and on.

Bye and bye it met a man.

"Good day!" said the man.

"Good day!" said the Pancake.

"Oh! wait a moment," said the man. "I want a bite of you."

"Oh, no," said the Pancake. "I've just rolled away from seven hungry children, a Mother, a Father, and I'll roll away from you, Manny-Panny." It rolled on and on and on.

Then it met a hen.

"Good day!" said the Hen.

"Good day!" said the Pancake.

"Wait a moment," said the Hen. "I want a bite of you."

"Oh, no," said the Pancake. "I've rolled away from seven hungry children, a Mother, a Father, Manny-Panny, and I'll roll away from you, Henny-Penny," and it rolled on and on and on until it met a cock.

"Good day!" said the Cock.

"Good day!" said the Pancake.

"Oh! wait a moment," said the Cock. "I want a bite of you."

"Oh, no," said the Pancake, "I've just rolled away from seven hungry children, a Mother, a Father, Manny-Panny, Henny-Penny, and I'll roll away from you, Cocky-Locky." And it rolled on and on and on until it met a Duck.

"Good day!" said the Duck.

"Good day!" said the Pancake.

"Oh, wait a moment," said the Duck. "I want a bite of you."

"Oh, no," said the Pancake. "I've just rolled away from seven hungry children, a Mother, a Father, Manny-Panny, Henny-Penny, Cocky-Locky, and I'll roll away from you, Ducky-Lucky." And it rolled on and on and on until it met a goose.

"Good day!" said the Goose.

"Good day!" said the Pancake.

"Oh! wait a moment," said the Goose. "I want a bite of you."

"Oh, no," said the Pancake. "I've rolled away from seven hungry children, a Mother, a Father, Manny-Panny, Henny-Penny, Cocky-Locky, Ducky-Lucky, and I'll roll away from you, Goosey-Poosey." And it rolled on and on and on until it met a Gander.

"Good day!" said the Gander.

"Good day!" said the Pancake.

"Oh! wait a moment," said the Gander. "I want a bite of you."

"Oh, no," said the Pancake. "I've rolled away from seven hungry children, a Mother, a Father, Manny-Panny, Henny-Penny, Cocky-Locky, Ducky-Lucky,

Goosey-Poosey, and I'll roll away from you, Gander-Pander," and it rolled on and on and on.

After it rolled a very long way it met a pig.

"Good day!" said the Pig.

"Good day!" said the Pancake.

"Oh! said the Pig, "you need not hurry along so fast, as we are going the same way, we may just as well travel along together. Besides," said the Pig, "it is not very safe in this wood; someone might eat you."

"Very well," said the Pancake, and they traveled on side by side.

All went well until they came to a stream flowing through the wood. It was all very well for the Pig because he was so fat that he could swim across. But poor Pancake could not get over.

"I know what you can do," said the Pig, "just roll upon my snout and I will carry you across."

The Pancake rolled up on the Pig's snout.

"Ouf! Ouf!" went the Pig and down went the Pancake.

The Three Bears

THE THREE BEARS

ONCE upon a time there were three Bears. They lived in a little house in the wood.

One was a great Huge Bear, one was a Middle Sized Bear and one was a Little Wee Bear.

Each had a bowl for his porridge: a great large bowl for the great Huge Bear, a middle sized one for the Middle Sized Bear, and a cunning little one for the Little Wee Bear.

Each had his own chair: a great, large chair for the great Huge Bear, a middle sized one for the

Middle Sized Bear, and a nice little one for the Little Wee Bear.

Each had his own bed: a large one for the great Huge Bear, a middle sized one for the Middle Sized Bear, and a little wee one for the Little Wee Bear.

One morning bright and early, the Middle Sized Bear made some porridge for breakfast, and as it was very hot, poured it into the bowl to cool. While it was cooling the three Bears went out for a walk in the wood.

Presently a little girl by the name of Golden Locks came up to the house of the Three Bears. First she looked in at the window and then she peeped

in at the key hole. When she found that every one was away, she lifted up the latch and walked in.

Golden Locks was quite hungry after her walk and was very happy to see the three bowls of nice porridge on the table.

First she tasted the great Huge Bear's porridge and that was too hot. She tasted the Middle Sized Bear's porridge and that was too cool. And then she tasted the Little Wee Bear's porridge and that was just right. So she ate it all up.

Feeling a little tired, she looked around and saw three chairs. First she sat in the great Huge Bear's chair; that was too high. She sat in the Middle Sized Bear's chair; that was too broad. Then she sat in

the Little Wee Bear's chair; that was just right. So she sat there until the chair went to pieces.

She went into the bedroom. First she tried the great Huge Bear's bed; that was too hard. She tried the Middle Sized Bear's bed; that was too soft.

Then she tried the Little Wee Bear's bed; that was just right, and she drew up the covers and fell fast asleep.

By this time the Bears decided to come home for their breakfast.

When they entered the house and went over to the table, the great Huge Bear, in his great, rough voice, said, "Somebody has been tasting my porridge."

Then the Middle Sized Bear, in her Middle Sized voice, said, "Somebody has been tasting my porridge."

And the Little Wee Bear, in his little wee voice,

LOIS LENSKI

said, "Somebody has been tasting my porridge, and has eaten it all up!"

The three Bears knew there was somebody in the house. Going over to their chairs, the great Huge Bear, in his great rough voice, said, "Somebody has been sitting in my chair."

The Middle Sized Bear, in her middle sized voice, said, "Somebody has been sitting in my chair!"

And then the Little Wee Bear, in his little wee voice, said, "Somebody has been sitting in my chair and broke it all down!"

The three Bears hurried into their bedroom. The great Huge Bear went over to his bed and, in his great loud voice, said, "Somebody has been in my bed!"

The Middle Sized Bear in her middle sized voice, said, "Somebody has been in my bed!"

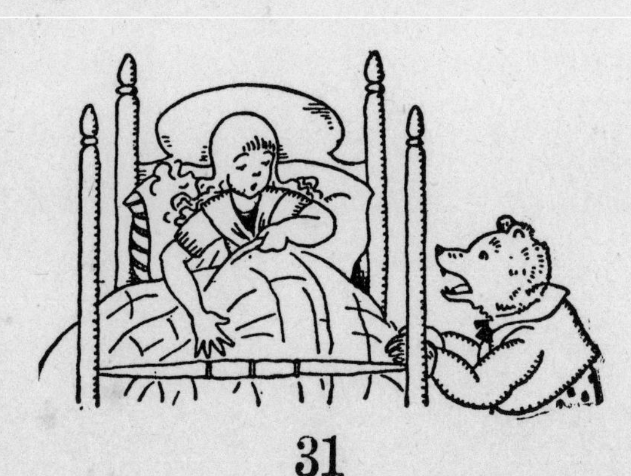

The Little Wee Bear in his little wee voice, said, "Somebody has been in my bed and here she is!"

With that Golden Locks opened her eyes and when she saw the three Bears standing by the bed looking at her, she jumped quickly out of the Little Wee Bear's bed—ran out of the house and through the wood as fast as she could. The three Bears never saw her again.

The Three Billy Goats Gruff

The three BILLY GOATS GRUFF

ONCE upon a time there were three Billy goats and their name was Gruff.

They were going up the mountain to get fat.

On their way up they had to cross a bridge and under this bridge there lived a Troll, with eyes as big as saucers and a nose as long as a broomstick.

The Billy goats did not know that the Troll lived there.

First of all came Little Billy Goat Gruff. He went trip-trap-trip-trap over the bridge.

The Troll poked up his head and said, "Who goes trip-trap-trip-trap-trip-trap over my bridge?"

The Little Billy goat said, "It is I, Little Billy Goat Gruff, and I'm going up the mountain to get fat."

"Oh, no, you're not," said the Troll, "because I'm going to eat you."

"Oh," said Little Billy Goat Gruff, "you wouldn't eat me, would you? I am so small, just wait for my brother, second Billy Goat Gruff and you eat him. He is much larger than I."

"Very well," said the Troll. "Be off with you," and trip-trap-trip-trap-trip-trap went Little Billy Goat Gruff.

Presently along came Second Billy Goat Gruff, and he went trip-trap! trip-trap! trip-trap! over the bridge. The Troll poked up his head and said, "Who goes trip-trap! trip-trap! trip-trap! over my bridge?"

The Second Billy Goat Gruff tried to make his voice sound very weak too, and he said, "It is I, Second Billy Goat Gruff, and I am going up to the mountain to get fat."

"Oh, no, you're not," said the Troll, "because I'm going to eat you."

LOIS LENSKI

Then the Second Billy Goat said, "Oh, you wouldn't eat me, would you? I am so small. You wait for my brother, Great Billy Goat Gruff, and you eat him. He is much larger than I."

"Very well then," said the Troll, "be off with you;" and trip-trap! trip-trap! trip-trap! went Second Billy Goat Gruff.

Last of all came Great Billy Goat Gruff. Oh, he was a great, large fellow. His great shaggy fur hung down to his feet. He had two large horns coming out of his forehead. When he walked the bridge just shook. He went Trip-Trop! Trip-Trop! Trip-Trop! "Oh!" went the bridge, he was so heavy.

The Troll poked up his head and said, "Who goes Trip-Trop! Trip-Trop! Trip-Trop! over my bridge?"

The Great Billy Goat stood there and said, "It is I, Great Billy Goat Gruff, and I'm going up the mountain to get fat."

"Oh, no, you're not," said the Troll, "because I am going to eat you."

"Come along then," said the Great Billy Goat Gruff, and up came the Troll. The Great Billy Goat caught him with his two horns and tossed him way

up in the sky. That was the end of the Troll; and Trip-Trop! Trip-Trop! Trip-Trop! away he went over the bridge. By this time the three Billy goats are so fat that they couldn't come back even though they wanted to. So

"Snip Snap Snout
My tale is out."

Peter Rabbit

PETER RABBIT

ONCE upon a time there were four little Rabbits. Their names were
FLOPSY,
MOPSY,
COTTON-TAIL,
and PETER.
They lived with their Mother in a sand-bank, underneath the root of a very big fir tree.

"Now, my dears," said old Mrs. Rabbit one morning, "you may go into the fields or down the lane, but don't go into Mr. McGregor's garden. Your

Father had an accident there; he was put in a pie by Mrs. McGregor."

"Now, run along, and don't get into mischief. I am going out."

Then old Mrs. Rabbit took a basket and her umbrella, and went through the woods to the baker's. She bought a loaf of brown bread and five currant buns.

Flopsy, Mopsy, and Cotton-tail, who were good little bunnies, went down the lane to gather blackberries; but Peter, who was very naughty, ran straight away to Mr. McGregor's garden, and squeezed under the gate!

First he ate some lettuce, then some French beans; and then he ate some radishes; then, feeling rather ill, he went to look for some parsley.

LOIS
LENSKI

But around the end of the cucumber frame, whom should he meet but Mr. McGregor!

Mr. McGregor was on his hands and knees planting young cabbages, but he jumped up and ran after Peter, waving a rake and calling out, "Stop thief!"

Peter was most dreadfully frightened; he rushed all over the garden, for he had forgotten the way back to the gate.

He lost one of his shoes among the cabbages, and the other shoe amongst the potatoes.

After losing them, he ran on four legs and went faster, and I think he might have escaped if he had not unfortunately run into a gooseberry net, where he was caught by the large buttons on his jacket. It was a blue jacket with brass buttons, quite new.

Peter gave himself up for lost, and shed big tears; but his sobs were overheard by some friendly sparrows, who flew to him in great excitement, and implored him to try and help himself.

Mr. McGregor came up with a sieve, which he intended to pop upon the top of Peter; but Peter wriggled out just in time, leaving his jacket behind him.

He rushed into the tool-shed, and jumped into a can. It would have been a beautiful thing to hide in, if it had not had so much water in it.

Mr. McGregor was quite sure that Peter was somewhere in the tool shed, perhaps hidden underneath a flower-pot. He began to turn them over carefully, looking under each.

Presently Peter sneezed—"Kertyschoo!" Mr. McGregor was after him in no time, and tried to put his foot upon Peter, who jumped out of a window, upsetting three plants. The window was too small for Mr. McGregor, and he was tired running after Peter. He went back to his work.

Peter sat down to rest; he was out of breath and trembling with fright and he had not the least idea which way to go. Also he was very damp from sitting in that can.

After a time he began to wander about, going lippity-lippity—not very fast, looking all around.

He found a door in a wall; but it was locked, and there was no room for a fat little rabbit to squeeze underneath.

An old mouse was running in and out over the stone door-step, carrying peas and beans to her family in the wood. Peter asked her the way to the gate, but she had such a large pea in her mouth that she could not answer. She only shook her head at him. Peter began to cry.

Then he tried to find his way straight across the garden, but he became more and more puzzled. Presently he came to a pond where Mr. McGregor filled his water-cans. A white cat was staring at some gold-fish; she sat very, very still, but now and then the tip of her tail twitched as if it were alive.

Peter thought it best to go away without speaking to her; he had heard about cats from his cousin, little Benjamin Bunny.

He went back towards the tool-shed, but suddenly, quite close to him, he heard the noise of a hoe—scr-r-ritch, scratch, scratch, scritch. Peter scuttered underneath the bushes. But presently as nothing happened, he came out, and climbed upon a wheelbarrow, and peeped over. The first thing he saw was Mr. McGregor hoeing onions. His back was turned towards Peter, and beyond him was the gate; Peter got down very quietly off the wheel-barrow, and started running as fast as he could go, along a straight walk, behind some black-currant bushes.

Mr. McGregor caught sight of him at the corner, but Peter did not care. He slipped underneath the gate, and was safe at last in the wood outside the garden.

Mr. McGregor hung up the little jacket and the shoes as a scare-crow to frighten the blackbirds.

Peter never stopped running nor looked behind until he reached home, the big fir tree.

He was so tired that he flopped down upon the

nice soft sand on the floor of the rabbit-hole, and closed his eyes. His Mother was busy cooking; she wondered what he had done with his clothes. It was the second little jacket and pair of shoes that Peter had lost in a fortnight; I am sorry to say that Peter was not very well during the evening.

His Mother put him to bed, and made some camomile tea, and gave him a dose of it: "One tablespoonful to be taken at bed-time."

But Flopsy, Mopsy, and Cotton-Tail had bread and milk and blackberries for supper.

The Three Pigs

THE THREE PIGS

ONCE upon a time there was a mother pig, who had three little pigs. As she was very poor, she had to send them into the world to seek their fortunes.

The first little pig was walking down the road and he met a man with a bundle of straw.

"Please, man," said the little pig, "could you give me that straw to build a house?"

"Why, certainly," said the man, and he gave the little pig the bundle of straw.

The little pig started right to work and built himself a lovely little house.

Presently along came an old wolf and, seeing the little pig inside the house, knocked at the door and said, "Little Pig! Little Pig! Let me come in!"

"Oh, no," said the pig, "by the hair on my chinny chin chin."

"Then," said the wolf, "I'll huff and I'll puff and I'll blow your house in!"

So he huffed and he puffed and down came the house and he ate up the little pig.

The second little pig started out to seek his fortune and he met a man with a load of sticks.

"Oh, please, man," said the little pig, "could you give me those sticks to build a house?"

'Why, certainly," said the man, and gave the little pig the sticks. Then the second little pig built himself a little house.

Just after he had finished it, along came the wolf and said, "Little Pig! Little Pig! Let me come in!"

"Oh, no!" said the pig, "bythe hair on my chinny chin chin."

"Then," said the wolf, "I'll huff and I'll puff and I'll blow your house in."

So he huffed and he puffed and down came the house and he ate up the little pig.

The third little pig started out to seek his fortune. He met a man with a load of bricks.

"Oh, please, man," said the pig, "could you give me those bricks to build a house?"

"Why, certainly," said the man, and he gave the bricks to the little pig.

The third little pig worked very hard and built a little house. Again the old wolf came and said: "Little Pig! Little Pig! Let me come in!"

"Oh, no!" said the pig, "by the hair of my chinny chin chin."

"Then," said the wolf, "I'll huff and I'll puff and I'll blow your house in."

So he huffed and he puffed and he puffed and he huffed but he could not blow this house in because it was made of bricks.

The wolf made up his mind to get this little pig one way or another. So he said, "Oh, little pig, I know where to find the loveliest sweet turnips."

"Where?" asked the little pig.

"Oh, in Farmer Smith's farm," said the wolf, "and if you are ready tomorrow morning at six o'clock I shall call for you and we shall go there together and get some for our dinner."

The little pig started off at five o'clock the next morning and was home eating his breakfast when the wolf knocked at the door, and said, "Are you ready, little pig?"

"Ready?" said the little pig. "Why, how late you are! I have been there already, and have a nice basket of turnips for my dinner."

When the wolf heard this he was very angry, but, pretending he didn't care, said sweetly, "Oh, little pig, I know where there is a tree of juicy red apples."

LOIS LENSKI

"Where?" asked the little pig.

"Oh, in Farmer Brown's garden," replied the wolf. "If you are ready to-morrow morning at five o'clock, I shall call for you and we shall go there together."

The little pig was up the next morning at four o'clock and scampered off to find the apples, hoping to be home before the wolf came. But the wolf had been fooled once by the little pig, so he also started off at four o'clock and when he found that the little pig was not at home he went right over to Farmer Brown's garden. The little pig was just ready to come down from the tree with a large bag of red apples when he saw the wolf looking up at him.

"Oh, dear," thought the little pig, "what shall I do?"

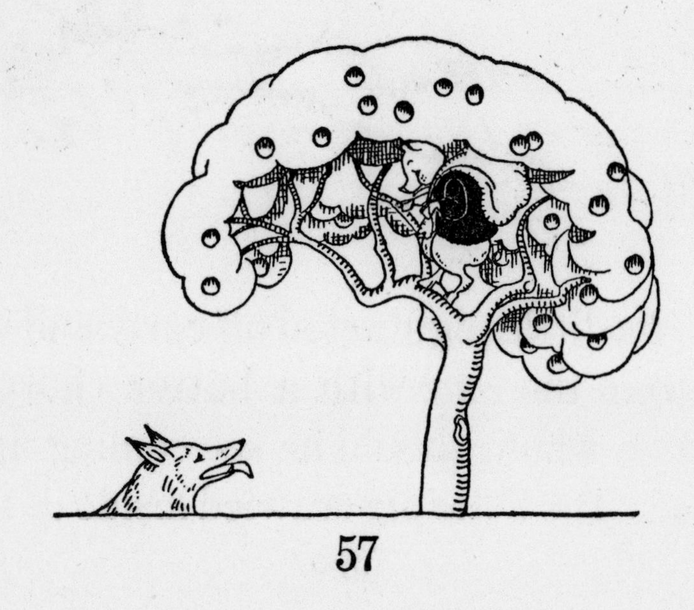

The wolf called up to him, “Good morning, little pig, my, but you are up early! How are the apples?”

“Delicious,” said the little pig, “wait a moment and I will throw one down to you.” He threw it so far that he was safely home before the wolf found the apple.

The wolf was furious to think that the little pig had played another trick upon him, but he went back to the little pig’s house and said: “How would you like to go to the Fair, little pig? If you are ready this afternoon at three o’clock I shall call for you and we shall go together.”

As usual, the little pig started off early and was coming home from the Fair with a butter churn he had bought, when whom should he see coming up the hill but the wolf. The little pig crawled inside of the churn to hide. Just as he did this, the churn slipped and rolled over and over down the hill.

This strange sight frightened the wolf so much that he ran straight home.

The next day he came to the little pig's house and said, "Little pig, I am so sorry I missed you yesterday, but just as I was coming for you, something very strange came rolling down the hill and it frightened me so that I ran straight home."

"Ha! Ha!" laughed the little pig. "I frightened you, did I? Why, I was inside the churn."

When the wolf heard this, he made up his mind to eat the little pig at once. Up on top of the house he crawled, and started down the chimney, after the little pig.

Then the little pig made a great, blazing fire and filled a large kettle of water. Just as the wolf came tumbling down the chimney, the little pig lifted the cover off the kettle and in fell the wolf. The little pig quickly put the cover on again and that was the end of the wolf.

As for the little pig, he lived happily ever after.

The Little Red Hen and the Grain of Wheat

The LITTLE RED HEN and the GRAIN of WHEAT

ONE day the Little Red Hen was scratching in the farmyard when she found a grain of wheat.

"Who will plant the wheat?" said she.

"Not I," said the duck.

"Not I," said the cat.

"Not I," said the dog.

"Very well then," said the Little Red Hen, "I will." So she planted the grain of wheat.

After some time the wheat grew tall and ripe.

"Who will cut the wheat?" asked the Little Red Hen.

"Not I," said the duck.

"Not I," said the cat.

"Not I," said the dog.

"Very well then, I will," said the Little Red Hen. So she cut the wheat.

"Now," she said, "who will thresh the wheat?"

"Not I," said the duck.

"Not I," said the cat.

"Not I," said the dog.

"Very well then, I will," said the Little Red Hen. So she threshed the wheat.

When the wheat was threshed, she said, "Who will take the wheat to the mill to have it ground into flour?"

"Not I," said the duck.

"Not I," said the cat.

"Not I," said the dog.

"Very well then, I will," said the Little Red Hen. So she took the wheat to the mill.

When the wheat was ground into flour, she said, "Who will make this flour into bread?"

"Not I," said the duck.

"Not I," said the cat.

"Not I," said the dog.

"Very well then, I will," said the Little Red Hen, and then baked a lovely loaf of bread.

Then she said, "Who will eat the bread?"

"Oh! I will," said the duck.

"Oh! I will," said the cat.

"Oh! I will," said the dog.

"Oh, no, you won't!" said the Little Red Hen. "I will." And she called her chicks and shared the bread with them.

Little Black Sambo

LITTLE BLACK SAMBO

ONCE upon a time there was a little boy and his name was Little Black Sambo.

His mother was called Black Mumbo.

His father was called Black Jumbo.

Black Mumbo made him a beautiful little Red Coat, and a beautiful little pair of Blue Trousers.

Black Jumbo went to the Bazaar and bought him a beautiful little Green Umbrella and a lovely pair of Purple Shoes with Crimson Soles and Crimson Linings.

And then wasn't Little Black Sambo grand!

He put on his fine clothes and went for a walk in the Jungle. By and by he met a Tiger.

The Tiger growled at him and said, "Little Black Sambo, I'm going to eat you up."

Little Black Sambo said, "Oh, please, Mr. Tiger, don't eat me up, and I'll give you my beautiful little Red Coat."

So the Tiger said, "Very well, I won't eat you this time, but you must give me your beautiful Red Coat."

Little Black Sambo took off his beautiful Red Coat and the Tiger put it on and off he went with his head in the air, saying, "Now I'm the Grandest Tiger in the Jungle."

Little Black Sambo went still further and he met another tiger.

The Tiger growled at him and said, "Little Black Sambo, I'm going to eat you up!"

Little Black Sambo said, "Oh, please, Mr. Tiger, don't eat me up, and I'll give you my beautiful Blue Trousers."

Then the Tiger said, "Very well, I won't eat you up this time, but you must give me your beautiful little Blue Trousers."

Little Black Sambo took off his beautiful little Blue Trousers, and the Tiger put them on, and off he went with his head in the air, saying, "Now I'm the Grandest Tiger in the Jungle."

Little Black Sambo went still further and he met another Tiger.

The Tiger growled at him and said, "Little Black Sambo, I'm going to eat you up."

"Little Black Sambo said, "Oh, please, Mr. Tiger, don't eat me up, and I'll give you my lovely Purple Shoes with Crimson Soles and Crimson Linings."

But the Tiger said, "Oh, no! your Shoes wouldn't

do me any good, I have four feet and you have only two. I'm going to eat you up."

Then Little Black Sambo said, "You could put them on your ears."

"So I could," said the Tiger, "that's a very good idea; I won't eat you this time."

Little Black Sambo took off his lovely Purple Shoes with Crimson Soles and Crimson Linings and the Tiger put one on each ear, and off he went with his head in the air saying, "Now I'm the Grandest Tiger in the Jungle."

Little Black Sambo went still further and he met another Tiger.

The Tiger growled at him and said, "Little Black Sambo, I'm going to eat you up."

Little Black Sambo said, "Oh, please, Mr. Tiger, don't eat me up, and I'll give you my beautiful Green Umbrella."

The Tiger said, "Oh, no! your umbrella wouldn't do me any good, I couldn't carry it. You see, I have to use my four feet to walk on. I'm going to eat you up."

"Oh!" said Little Black Sambo, "I know what you

could do. You could tie a knot in your tail and carry it that way."

"So I could," said the Tiger.

He tied a knot in his tail and slipped the Umbrella through it, and off he went with his head in the air, saying, "Now I'm the Grandest Tiger in the Jungle."

Poor Little Black Sambo had lost all his fine clothes and he started home crying.

By and by he heard a terrible noise that sounded like Gr-r-r r-r-r rrrrrr. It grew louder and louder.

"Oh! dear," said Little Black Sambo, "what shall I do? Here come the Tigers to eat me up!"

He ran and hid behind a Palm Tree. After a while he peeped around it to see what the Tigers were doing.

There were all the Tigers fighting. Each said that he was the Grandest Tiger in the Jungle. At last they grew so angry that they took off their fine clothes and began to fight again.

They came rolling and tumbling right to the foot of the tree where Little Black Sambo was hiding. Little Black Sambo jumped quickly behind his little Green Umbrella. The Tigers went round and round the Tree, one Tiger with another Tiger's tail in his mouth.

"Little Black Sambo called out, "Tigers, don't you want your clothes any more? If you don't want them, say so, and I'll take them back."

But the Tigers wouldn't let go of each other's tails. All that they said was, "Gr-r-r-r-r-r rrrrrrr."

Then Little Black Sambo put on his fine clothes and walked off.

When the Tigers saw this they were very, very angry, but they wouldn't let go of each other's tails. They ran round and round the Tree, faster and faster, trying to eat each other up. Finally they ran so fast that they just melted away and there was

nothing left of them but melted butter around the foot of the Tree.

That evening Black Jumbo was coming home from work with a large Brass Bowl in his arms. When he saw what was left of the Tigers, he said,

"Oh! what nice melted butter! I'll take some home for Black Mumbo to cook with." So he filled up the big Brass Bowl and carried it home to Black Mumbo.

When Black Mumbo saw the melted butter she was very much pleased.

"Now," she said, "we will have Pancakes for supper!"

So she mixed up some flour and eggs and milk and sugar and the butter, and made a huge platter of lovely Pancakes.

Then they all sat down to supper. Black Mumbo ate twenty-seven Pancakes because she made them. Black Jumbo ate fifty-five Pancakes because he brought the butter home, but Little Black Sambo ate one hundred and sixty-nine Pancakes because he was so hungry.

The Cock, The Mouse and the little Red Hen

THE COCK, THE MOUSE *and the* LITTLE RED HEN

ONCE upon a time, there was a hill, and on the hill there was a pretty little house.

It had one little green door, and four little windows with green shutters, and in it there lived

A COCK and A MOUSE and A LITTLE RED HEN.

On another hill close by there was another little house. It was very ugly. It had a door that wouldn't shut, and two broken windows, and all the paint was off the shutters. In this house there lived

A BOLD BAD FOX and FOUR LITTLE FOXES.

One morning these four bad little foxes came to the big bad Fox and said, "Oh, Father, we are so hungry!"

"We had nothing to eat yesterday," said one.

"And scarcely anything the day before," said another.

"And only a half a chicken the day before that," said a third.

"And only two little ducks the day before that," said the fourth.

The big bad Fox shook his head for a long time, for he was thinking. At last he said in a big rough voice, "On the hill over there I see a house. And in that house there lives a Cock."

"And a Mouse," screamed two of the little foxes.

"And a little Red Hen," screamed the other two.

"And they are nice and fat," went on the big bad Fox.

"This very day, I will take my great sack, and I will go up that hill and in at that door, and into my sack I will put the Cock, and the Mouse, and the little Red Hen."

"I will make a fire to roast the Cock," said one little fox.

"I will put on the sauce-pan to boil the Hen," said the second.

"And I will get the fryingpan to fry the Mouse," said the third.

"And I will have the biggest helping when they are all cooked," said the fourth, who was the greediest of all.

Then the four little foxes jumped for joy and the big bad Fox went to get his sack ready to start upon his journey.

But what was happening to the Cock, and the Mouse and the little Red Hen all of this time?

Well, sad to say, the Cock and the Mouse got out of bed on the wrong side that morning. The Cock said the day was too hot, and the Mouse said that the day was too cold.

They came grumbling down to the kitchen, where

the good little Red Hen, looking as bright as a sunbeam, was bustling about.

"Who will get some sticks to make the fire?" she asked.

"I shan't," said the Cock.

"I shan't," said the Mouse.

"Then I will do it myself," said the little Red Hen.

So off she ran to get the sticks.

"Now who will fill the kettle from the spring?" she asked.

"I shan't," said the Cock.

"I shan't," said the Mouse.

"Then I will do it myself," said the little Red Hen.

And off she went to fill the kettle.

"Now who will get the breakfast ready?" she asked as she put the kettle on to boil.

"I shan't," said the Cock.

"I shan't," said the Mouse.

"Then I will do it myself," said the little Red Hen.

All during breakfast the Cock and the Mouse quarreled and grumbled.

The Cock upset the milk jug and the Mouse scattered crumbs upon the floor.

"Who will clear away the breakfast?" asked the poor little Red Hen, hoping they would soon leave off being cross.

"I shan't," said the Cock.

"I shan't," said the Mouse.

"Then I will do it myself," said the little Red Hen.

So she cleared everything away, swept up the crumbs, and brushed up the fireplace.

"Now, who will help me to make the beds?"

"I shan't," said the Cock.

"I shan't," said the Mouse.

"Then I will do it myself," said the little Red Hen.

And she tripped away upstairs.

The lazy Cock and the Mouse each sat down in a comfortable armchair by the fire, and soon fell fast asleep.

Now the bad Fox had crept up the hill, and into the garden, and if the Cock and the Mouse had not been asleep, they would have seen his sharp eyes peeping in at the window.

"Rat, Tat, Tat, Rat tat tat," the Fox knocked at the door.

"Who can that be?" asked the Mouse, half opening his eyes.

"Go and look for yourself, if you want to know," said the rude Cock.

"Perhaps it is the Postman, and he may have a letter for me," thought the Mouse to himself. So without waiting to see who it was, he lifted the latch and opened the door.

As soon as he opened it, in walked the big Fox with a cruel smile upon his face.

"Oh! oh! oh!" squeaked the Mouse, as he tried to run up the chimney.

"Doodle doodle do!" screamed the Cock, as he jumped on the back of the biggest arm-chair.

The Fox only laughed and without more ado pop into his bag went the Mouse and pop into his bag went the Cock, and the little Red Hen came running downstairs to see what all the noise was about, and pop into the bag went the little Red Hen.

Then the Fox took a long piece of string out of his pocket, and wound it round and round and round

LOIS LENSKI

the mouth of the sack, and tied it very tight indeed. Then he threw the sack over his back and off he started down the hill.

The sun was very hot and soon Mr. Fox began to feel that his sack was heavy and at last he thought he would lie down under a tree and go to sleep for a while. He threw the sack down with a big bump and very soon fell fast asleep.

Snore, snore, snore, went the Fox.

As soon as the little Red Hen heard this she took out her scissors and began to snip a hole in the sack, just large enough for the Mouse to creep through.

"Quick," she whispered to the Mouse, "run as fast as you can and bring back a stone just as large as yourself."

Out scampered the Mouse and soon came back dragging the stone after him.

"Push it in here," said the little Red Hen, and he pushed it in in a twinkling.

Then the little Red Hen snipped away at the hole, until it was large enough for the Cock to get through.

"Quick," she said, "run just as fast as you can, and bring back a stone just as big as yourself."

Out flew the Cock, and soon came back quite out of breath, with a big stone, which he pushed into the sack too.

Then the little Red Hen popped out, found a stone just as big as herself, and pushed it in.

Then she put on her thimble, took out her needle and thread, and sewed up the hole as quickly as ever she could.

When it was done, the Cock and the Mouse and the little Red Hen ran home very fast, shut the doors after them, drew the bolts, shut down the shutters, drew down the blinds, and felt quite safe.

The bad Fox lay fast asleep under the tree for some time, but at last he woke up.

"Dear, dear," he said, rubbing his eyes, and then looking at the long shadows on the grass, "how late it is getting. I must hurry home."

The bad Fox went rumbling and groaning down the hill, until he came to the stream. Splash! In went one foot. Splash! In went the other, but the stones in the sack were so heavy that the very next step down tumbled Mr. Fox into a deep pool. And then the fishes carried him off to their caves and kept him there, so he was never seen again. And the four greedy little foxes had to go to bed that night without any supper.

But the Cock and the Mouse never grumbled again. They lit the fire, filled the kettle, they laid the breakfast, and did all the work, while the good little Red Hen had a holiday, and sat resting in the big armchair.

No foxes ever troubled them again, and for all I know they are still living happily in the little house with the green door and the green shutters which stands on the hill.

The Travels of a Fox

The TRAVELS *of* A FOX

NE day a Fox was digging behind a stump of an old tree, and found a Bumble-bee. He put it in his bag, threw his bag over his shoulder and traveled.

By and by he came to a house, he knocked at the door and said to the Mistress, "May I leave my bag here while I go to Squintum's?"

"Why, certainly," said the Woman.

"Well, then," said the Fox, "be very careful and do not look in this bag," and off he went.

The old Fox was scarcely around the corner when the Woman said, "I wonder what can be in the bag that the old Fox is so very careful of. I think I will look in and see."

So she opened the bag, just a wee bit, and out flew the Bumble-bee and her Rooster ate it.

In a short time the Fox came back, and looking in his bag, he said, "Where is my Bumble-bee?"

"Oh!" said the Woman, "I am so sorry, but I just opened your bag a wee bit to see what was in it, and your Bumble-bee flew right out and my Rooster ate it."

"Very well, I must have your Rooster," said the Fox. So he put the Rooster in his bag, threw the bag over his shoulder and traveled.

He soon came to another house, knocked at the door, and said to the Mistress, "May I leave my bag here while I go to Squintum's?"

"Yes, if you wish," said she.

"Then be very careful and do not open the bag," said the Fox and trotted off.

But he was only around the corner, when the Woman said, "Now, I wonder what can be in the bag that the old Fox is so very careful of. I think I will look in and see."

So she untied the string and looked in and out flew the Rooster and her Pig ate it.

Back came the Fox, and looking in his bag, he said, "Where is my Rooster?"

"Oh!" said the Woman, "I am very sorry indeed, but I opened the bag just to see what was in it and your Rooster flew out and my Pig ate it.

"Very well then, I must have your Pig," said the Fox.

So he caught the little Pig, put it in his bag, threw the bag over his shoulder and traveled.

Going up to the next house, he knocked at the

door and said to the Mistress, "May I leave my bag here while I go to Squintum's?"

"Why, yes, you may," said the Woman.

"Then be very careful and do not open it," said the Fox, and off he went.

But the Fox hadn't gone very far when the Woman said, "I wonder what can be in that bag that the old Fox is so very careful of. I think I will look in the bag and see."

With that she opened the bag and out jumped the Pig squealing, and the Woman's Ox ran after it and caught it, tossed it upon his horns, and that was the end of the Pig.

When the Fox came back he looked at his bag, and knew at once that his Pig was gone; so he said, "Where is my Pig?"

"Oh!" said the Woman, "I am sorry but I just opened your bag to see what was in it, and your Pig jumped out and my Ox ran after it and caught it, then tossed it upon his horns, and that was the end of your Pig."

"Well, if that's the case," said the Fox, "I must have your Ox."

LOIS LENSKI

So he put the Ox in his bag, threw the bag over his shoulder and traveled.

When he came to the next house, he knocked at the door, and said to the Mistress, "May I leave my bag here while I go to Squintum's?"

"Why, yes," said the Woman.

"Then be very careful," said the Fox, "and do not open it," and off he went.

When the Fox was out of sight, the Woman said: "I wonder what can be in the bag that the old Fox is so very careful of. I am sure that it will do no harm, if I just open it and look in."

So she untied the bag and out walked the Ox.

Now the Woman's little Boy was standing there, and he picked up a stick and drove the Ox over the hills and far away, then came running back home.

When the Fox came back and looked at his bag, he knew at once that his Ox was gone.

He said to the Woman, "Where is my Ox?"

"Oh!" said the Woman, "I am sorry, but I just opened your bag to see what was in it, and out walked your Ox, and my little Boy who is standing right here picked up a stick and drove it over the hills and far away."

"Very well, then," said the Fox, "I am sorry, but I must have your little Boy."

He put the little Boy into his bag and traveled. After a while he came to another house; he knocked at the door and said to the Mistress, "May I leave my bag here while I go to Squintum's?"

"You may if you wish," said she.

"Then be very careful and do not open it," said the Fox, and off he ran.

Now this Woman was baking ginger cookies, and oh, they smelled so good. Her children came running in from playing and one said:

"Please, Mother, give me a ginger cookie?"

Another said:

"Please, Mother, give me a ginger cookie?"

The little Boy in the bag smelled the ginger cookies too, and he called out:

"Please, Mammy, give me a ginger cookie?"

When the Woman heard this, she went right over to the bag, and opened it. Finding the little Boy, she took him out and put in the big black house Dog and quickly tied the bag again.

She then gave the little Boy and her Children some nice hot ginger cookies, which made them very happy indeed.

It was not very long before the old Fox came back. Seeing his bag tied up nice and tight, he did not stop to ask any questions but threw it over his shoulder and traveled.

After walking a long time, he came to a wood

and sat down under a tree to rest. He opened the bag to take a look at the little Boy and out jumped the big black house Dog and that was the end of the wicked old Fox.

Lazy Jack

LAZY JACK

ONCE upon a time there was a boy whose name was Jack, and he and his mother lived in a little house on a common.

They were very poor, and the mother earned her living by spinning. Jack, however, was so lazy that he would do nothing but bask in the sun in the hot weather and sit by the corner of the hearth in the winter-time. Because of this, they called him "Lazy Jack."

His mother could not get him to do anything for her; so at last she told him that if he did not begin to work for his porridge he would have to go out into the world and earn his living as he could.

This roused Jack, and he went out and hired himself for the next day to a neighboring farmer for a penny. But as he was on his way home, never having had any money before, he lost it in passing over a brook.

When he reached home and his mother found out what had happened, she said: "You stupid boy, you should have put it in your pocket."

"I'll do so another time," replied Jack.

Well, the next day Jack went out again and hired himself to a cow keeper, who gave him a jar of milk for his day's work. Jack took the jar and put it into the large pocket of his jacket, spilling it all long before he reached home.

"Dear me," said his mother; "you should have carried it on your head."

"I'll do so another time," said Jack.

So the following day Jack hired himself to a farmer, who agreed to give him a cream cheese for his services. In the evening Jack took the cream cheese and went home with it on his head.

By the time he reached home, the cheese was all spoilt, part of it being lost and part dripping down over his face.

"You stupid lad," said his mother, "you should have carried it carefully in your hands."

"I'll do so another time," replied Jack.

Now the next day Jack went out and hired himself to a baker, who would give him nothing for his work but a large tom-cat. Jack took the cat and began carrying it very carefully in his hands, but in a short time pussy scratched him so much that he was compelled to let it go.

When he reached home, his mother said to him:

"You silly fellow, you should have tied it with a string and dragged it along after you."

"I'll do so another time," said Jack.

So on the following day Jack hired himself to a butcher who rewarded him by the handsome present of a shoulder of mutton. Jack took the mutton, tied it to a string, and trailed it along after him in the dirt, so that by the time he reached home the meat was completely spoilt.

By this time his mother was quite out of patience with him, for the next day was Sunday, and she was obliged to do with cabbage for her dinner.

"You heedless boy," said she to her son; "you should have carried it on your shoulder."

"I'll do so another time," replied Jack.

Well, on Monday Jack went once more and hired himself to a cattle-keeper, who gave him a donkey for his trouble. Now, though Jack was strong, he found it hard to hoist the donkey on his shoulders, but at last he did it, and began walking home slowly with his prize.

It so happened that on his way home he passed a house where a rich man lived with his only daughter, a beautiful girl, but who had never laughed in her life, and so her father said that the man who could make her laugh could marry her.

Now this young lady happened to be looking out of the window when Jack was passing by with the donkey on his shoulders. The poor beast with its legs sticking up in the air was kicking hard and heehawing with all its might.

Well, the sight was so comical that she burst out into a great fit of laughter. Her father was overjoyed and kept his promise by marrying her to Jack, who was then made a rich gentleman.

They lived in a great house and Jack's mother lived with them in great happiness for the rest of her days.

LOIS
LENSKI

LOIS LENSKI

Mr. and Mrs. Vinegar

MR and MRS. VINEGAR

MR. AND MRS. VINEGAR lived in a Vinegar Bottle. It was the nicest vinegar bottle that anyone could have.

One day Mrs. Vinegar was busy sweeping, for she was a very good housewife, when suddenly she knocked the side of the Vinegar Bottle too hard, and klitter, klatter, down came the beautiful Vinegar Bottle over her head.

"Oh dear, oh dear," said Mrs. Vinegar, "what shall I do? What will Mr. Vinegar say?"

Out she ran to the garden, where Mr. Vinegar

was working. When Mr. Vinegar saw what had happened he said:

"My dear, don't feel so badly, there are other Vinegar Bottles. Let us take the door of our bottle, carry it on our backs, go out in the world and seek our fortune."

So Mr. and Mrs. Vinegar started out. They traveled all day and at night they came to a forest.

"Now," said Mr. Vinegar, "we will pull the door up into the tree and sleep on it."

After they were nicely settled for the night along came four robbers. They started to count their money, right under the very tree where Mr. and Mrs. Vinegar were sleeping.

One robber said, "Here are ten pounds for you, Bill."

"Here are ten pounds for you, Jack."

"Here are ten pounds for you, Tom."

At that Mr. Vinegar and Mrs. Vinegar awakened. They were so afraid and trembled so hard, that down came the door on top of the robbers' heads. At that the Robbers ran off leaving their money behind.

Mr. and Mrs. Vinegar stayed up in the tree until morning, because they were too frightened to come down.

When they came down and picked up the door—they found all the money.

Mr. Vinegar said, "Oh, my dear, our fortune is made."

Mrs. Vinegar said, "Now, Mr. Vinegar, take this money to the fair and buy a nice cow. The cow will give us milk, and we can churn the milk into butter, and sell the butter and buy eggs, and won't we be rich to the end of our days!"

Mr. Vinegar thought this was a very fine idea.

Off he started to the fair, jingling the money in his pocket.

Just as he entered the fair grounds, he happened to see a man with a beautiful red cow.

"Oh, dear," said Mr. Vinegar to the man with the red cow, "if I only had that cow I would be the happiest man alive."

"Why," said the man with the cow, "seeing you are a good friend of mine, I don't mind selling the cow to you for forty pounds."

So Mr. Vinegar handed over the forty pounds for the cow.

Instead of going straight home, he walked around the fair grounds showing off his cow. He had not gone very far, when he met a man playing bag-pipes. He played such beautiful music, that everyone followed him showering money into his hat.

"Oh, dear," said Mr. Vinegar, "what an easy way to make money. If only I had those bag-pipes I would be the happiest man alive."

"Well," said the man with the bag-pipes, "seeing you are such a good friend of mine, I don't mind giving you the bag-pipes for your cow."

"Oh, thank you," said Mr. Vinegar, and handed over his cow for the bag-pipes.

Poor Mr. Vinegar had never played bag-pipes before so instead of playing beautiful tunes, all he could play was squack-squack-squack. The boys and girls instead of showering pennies upon him laughed and shouted, I am sorry to say.

It was a cold November day and Mr. Vinegar's fingers grew very numb. On the road he met a man with a nice warm pair of red gloves.

"Oh, dear," said Mr. Vinegar, "if only I had those gloves I should be the happiest man alive."

"Why," said the man with the gloves, "seeing you are a good friend of mine, I do not mind giving the gloves to you for your bag-pipes."

"Fine," said Mr. Vinegar and put on the nice warm gloves.

He walked along happily for some time, humming as he went, but soon became so tired, he stumbled over rough bumps on the road. Looking up he saw a man coming toward him with a good stout stick in his hand.

"What use are these gloves to me," said Mr. Vinegar, "my feet ache from this rough road."

So he said to the man with the stick, "If only I had that stick I would be the happiest man alive."

"Well," said the man with the stick, "seeing you

are a good friend of mine, I do not mind giving you the stick for those gloves."

"Fine," said Mr. Vinegar, and traded the gloves for the stick.

Now a parrot was up in a tree and seeing what had happened, he called out,

"Oh, foolish Mr. Vinegar had forty pounds and bought a cow,

"Traded the cow for bag-pipes,

"Traded the bag-pipes for a pair of gloves,

"Traded the gloves for a stick that you could have cut from any tree,

"Foolish Mr. Vinegar."

Mr. Vinegar hearing this became so angry that he threw the stick into the tree.

When he came back to Mrs. Vinegar without money, cow, bag-pipes, gloves or stick, Mrs. Vinegar scolded him so hard that he was very sorry that he had not driven the cow straight home.

So this is the story of Mr. and Mrs. Vinegar.

The Elves and the Shoemaker

The ELVES *and the* SHOEMAKER

MANY years ago there lived an honest Shoemaker, but no matter how hard he worked, he was always very poor.

At last he had just enough leather left to make one pair of shoes. That night before going to bed, he cut off the leather and left it on his work-bench, thinking he would have an early start on his work when he awakened in the morning.

The next morning, much to his great surprise and joy, he found a beautiful pair of shoes perfectly made. He looked at them very carefully but could not find one false stitch.

He called his wife and they both wondered who could have done this, for the shoes were far better in every way than any the Shoemaker had ever made.

In a very short time a customer came in and, seeing the shoes, was so much pleased with them that he paid the Shoemaker twice as much as he would have for an ordinary pair.

With this money the Shoemaker bought enough leather to make two pairs of shoes.

That night he cut the leather as he had done the evening before. When morning came, there on the work-bench were two pairs of shoes, more beautifully made than the pair of the day before.

The Shoemaker and his wife were overjoyed at their good fortune. Presently other customers came. They too were delighted to find such splendid shoes and were willing to pay more than they had ever paid before.

With this money the Shoemaker was able to buy enough leather to make four pairs of shoes. He cut the leather as usual at night and in the morning, there on the work-bench were four pairs of shoes.

Buyers soon came in who were very glad to find such shoes as these.

So it kept on—whatever the Shoemaker would cut out at night would be found nicely finished in the morning.

The fame of his shoes spread far and wide and people came from all over the countryside to buy them.

By now the Shoemaker and his wife were very rich indeed.

One night just before Christmas, the Shoemaker and his wife were sitting before the fire talking about their unusual good fortune.

"I wonder," said the Shoemaker, "just who it is that comes at night and does my work for me. Whoever it is is very good indeed. Let us sit up to-night and watch."

His wife agreed, and that evening they left the candles burning and hid behind a curtain in a corner of the room.

Just at midnight two little elves came dancing in. Going over to the work-bench, they started to work at once. Their little fingers fairly flew and they stitched and hammered so fast that the watchers could scarcely believe their eyes.

Long before daylight they had finished their work. Then sweeping up all the scraps they left everything in perfect order.

When the Elves had gone, the Shoemaker's wife said: "These little people have been very good to us. Let us do something for them in return. I noticed how very thin their little jackets were. I shall make two little suits of clothes and two little warm caps. You make two little pairs of shoes."

They worked all day and that evening they put the little suits, caps and shoes on the bench, instead of the work they had been in the habit of leaving.

On the stroke of twelve, in came the little Elves. Over they went to the work-bench. Instead of finding the leather cut out ready to make into shoes, they found to their great joy two lovely little red suits and caps and two little pairs of shoes to match.

LOIS LENSKI

In the twinkle of an eye they were dressed. Then clapping their hands in high glee, they danced and whirled around the room and out the door over the snow.

The Shoemaker and his wife never saw them again, but from that time on they had everything they needed, and lived happily to the end of their days.

Bremen Town Musicians

BREMEN TOWN MUSICIANS

THERE was once a Donkey who had served his Master faithfully for many years. As he was growing old and was no longer able to carry the grain to the mill, his Master decided to sell him.

When the Donkey learned of this he made up his mind to run away. He took the road to Bremen Town, where he thought he would become a traveling musician. After walking some distance, he met a Dog panting by the roadside.

"What is the matter, my friend?" asked the Donkey. "You look very downhearted to-day."

"Indeed I am," replied the Dog. "Because I am not so young as I once was, my Master no longer wants me."

"Well," said the Donkey, "do not be unhappy about that; come with me to Bremen. I am going to be a traveling musician. You may beat the drum and I will bray."

The Dog agreed to this and off they trotted.

Presently they met a Cat sitting by the side of the road looking very sad indeed.

"Good morning, Tabby," said the Donkey. "Why are you grieving this bright summer day?"

"Oh, dearie me," replied the Cat, "now that I am getting old and prefer to sit by the fireplace instead of catching mice, my Mistress wants to find a new home for me. So I ran away, but how am I to live?"

"Come with us to Bremen Town," said the Donkey. "I know you are a splendid night singer. You may sing in our band."

The Cat joined them and away they went.

By and by they came to a farmyard. Sitting on the gate was a Cock, crowing with all his might.

"Good day, friend," said the Donkey. "Why are you crowing so loud?"

"Oh," said the Cock, "this morning I was crowing to let my Mistress know we were going to have fine weather, when out she came and told the cook that company was coming for supper and to make soup of me."

"Do not grieve over that," said the Donkey. "You have a fine voice; come with us to Bremen. We are going to be traveling musicians."

Off the four went, very happy and free-hearted.

As Bremen was a long way off, they had to spend a night in the wood. They looked around for a place to rest and at last found a fine large tree. The Dog and the Donkey lay down at the foot. The Cat found a resting place on a branch. The Cock flew up to the very top.

Before settling down for the night, the Cock looked around in all directions. Not far off he saw a light shining through the trees.

Calling down to his companions, he told them that there must be a house near by.

"If that is true," said the Donkey, "let us go there instead of spending the night here in the wood. I know that we would all like a more comfortable place to sleep."

They agreed and made their way out of the wood. The light grew brighter and brighter. At last they came to a house in which lived a band of robbers.

The Donkey, who was the tallest, looked in the window.

"What do you see?" asked the Cock.

"Oh," exclaimed the Donkey, "I see a table spread with the best of things to eat and drink, and a number of men sitting around eating and making merry."

"That is just the place for us," said the Cock.

After some talking they at last agreed upon a plan to drive the robbers away.

The Donkey placed his forefeet upon the window sill. The Dog jumped up on his back. The Cat climbed up on the Dog's shoulder. The Cock flew up on the Cat's head.

When the signal was given, the Donkey brayed, the Dog barked, the Cat mewed, and the Cock crowed. Then with a crash in they went through the window, the glass flying in all directions.

Hearing this terrible noise, the robbers jumped up and ran and ran until they were far from the house.

Left to themselves, the traveling musicians finished the supper, then putting out the lights, looked for places to sleep.

The Donkey found some hay near the gate. The Dog lay down behind the door. The Cat curled up in front of the fire, and the Cock flew up on the rafters of the house.

Now the robbers, who had been watching from a distance, seeing the house in darkness, decided that they had been too easily frightened.

The Captain ordered one of them to go back to the house to see what had happened.

He opened the door quietly, tiptoed across the room, picked up a candle, and stooped to light it from the bright coals burning in the fireplace. But what he thought were the coals proved to be the eyes of the cat shining in the darkness.

The Cat, not liking the joke, jumped up and scratched both his hands.

The Dog, who had been sleeping, awakened and sprang upon him as he rushed out of the door.

As he ran through the gate, the Donkey kicked him,

LOIS

and the Cock on top of the house crowed "Cock-a-doodle-do, Cock-a-doodle-do."

When the robber reached his companions, he told them that an old witch was in the house and that she scratched him when he tried to light a candle. A man with a knife stood behind a door and stabbed him as he went by. At the gate stood a monster who struck him with a club, and on top of the house was a judge who called out, "Bring the rascal up to me."

The robbers never went back to the house, but the traveling musicians liked it so much that they lived there the rest of their days.

Cinderella

CINDERELLA

ONCE upon a time there lived a girl who was as kind and gentle as she was beautiful.

As she had no home of her own, she worked for a woman who had two proud and haughty daughters.

Cinderella, the maid was called, because after her work was finished she sat by the fireplace in the kitchen raking the cinders, washed all the dishes and scrubbed the floors, and took care of the rooms of the two sisters. Their beds were made of the softest down. In their rooms were mirrors that reached from the floor to the ceiling, before which they admired themselves for hours at a time. Poor Cinderella slept on a bundle of straw in the garret and had only rags to dress in.

The two sisters were unkind to Cinderella, but no matter how harshly she was treated she was always sweet and good-tempered.

One day the King's son sent out invitations to a grand ball. The sisters were very happy indeed because they were invited to attend.

For days and days they talked of nothing but how they would dress and how beautiful they would look.

"I shall wear my red velvet gown trimmed with my fine point lace," said the elder sister.

The other sister said she would look far more beautiful in her gown of blue silk covered with gold brocade and studded with diamonds.

They quarreled so about their clothes that Cinderella tried to make peace between them. She offered to help them dress for the ball and promised to arrange their hair. The sisters were very willing indeed to accept her help because Cinderella had perfect taste. All this planning made extra work for Cinderella. She ironed their ruffles and fluted their frills, but never a word of praise or thanks did she receive for her efforts.

The evening of the ball as Cinderella was arranging the elder sister's hair, the sister said to her, "Cinderella, how would you like to go to the ball?"

"Oh," said Cinderella, "I would love to, but how could I go? I have nothing to wear."

"Of course," replied the sister, "you could not go. How the guests would laugh to see a cinder-maid at the ball."

After the sisters had gone Cinderella went into the kitchen and sat before the fire crying silently.

Suddenly, her fairy godmother appeared and seeing that she was weeping, said, "What is the matter, my child, why are you crying?"

"Oh," sobbed Cinderella, "I wish—I wish——"

"I know what you wish," said her fairy godmother. "You wish you could go to the ball, and so you shall."

"Now, dry your eyes and run into the garden and bring me a pumpkin."

Cinderella did as she was told and came running back with the largest pumpkin she could find.

The fairy godmother touched it with her wand and turned it into a beautiful golden coach. "Now for some horses," said her fairy godmother. "Bring me the mouse trap from the pantry." In the mouse trap were six little grey mice. The fairy godmother opened the trap and as each mouse ran out she touched it with her wand and it became a beautiful dapple grey horse.

"But what are we to do for a coachman?"

Cinderella thought she could find a rat in the rat trap. "That is a splendid idea, my dear," said the fairy godmother. Off Cinderella ran bringing back a trap in which were three large rats. The fairy godmother chose the largest and touching it with her wand turned it into a splendid coachman dressed in a suit of green trimmed with gold buttons.

They now needed footmen. The fairy godmother told Cinderella that she would find six lizards in the garden behind the watering pot. These she touched with her wand and six footmen with green suits trimmed with gold lace jumped up on the coach as if they had been doing this all their lives.

The fairy godmother then touched Cinderella with her wand. The ragged dress was changed into a gown of gold and silver cloth studded with pearls and other precious stones. On her feet were a pair of beautiful crystal slippers, the smallest in the world.

"Cinderella," said her fairy godmother, "you may now go to the ball, but remember, you are to leave before twelve o'clock or your coach will turn into a pumpkin, your horses into mice, your footmen into lizards, and your beautiful clothes back into rags."

Cinderella gaily promised to do as she was told

and stepping into her golden coach was quickly driven away.

When she reached the court-yard of the King's palace, word was sent to the Prince that a beautiful and unknown Princess had arrived.

The Prince came out to meet her and led her into the ball-room. As they entered the room, the musicians stopped playing, the guests stopped dancing, and everyone stood and wondered who the beautiful Princess could be. Even the King remarked to the Queen that he had never seen anyone quite so lovely in many years. The ladies of the court greatly admired her clothes and wondered just where they could find someone who could make just such a gown for them.

The Prince led her to the place of honor and then danced with her the entire evening.

At eleven o'clock a splendid supper was served.

Cinderella seated herself beside the sisters and spoke pleasantly to them. She also shared with them some of the fruit that the Prince had given to her.

The two sisters were very proud indeed to have the beautiful princess, whom the Prince had so highly honored, pay this marked attention to them. They did not, of course, recognize the little cinder-maid.

When the clock struck quarter to twelve, Cinderella arose and courtesied to the King and Queen. They invited her to attend another ball that was to be given the next evening. Then the Prince led her to her coach and stood looking after her as she was driven away.

Her fairy godmother was waiting for her when she reached home. Cinderella was overjoyed with everything that had happened. While she was telling her godmother about the ball, the sisters knocked at the door. Cinderella, rubbing her eyes as if she had been asleep for some time, opened the door.

"How late you are!" she said.

"Oh," replied the elder sister, "if you had been

to the ball and had seen the beautiful Princess we saw, you would not think it late."

"Who was she?" asked Cinderella.

"No one knew," said the younger sister, "not even the Prince. She was very lovely to us. She sat beside us at the supper and gave us some of the fruit the Prince had given her."

"How I would love to go to the ball to-morrow night, just to see this Princess!" said Cinderella. "Oh, my lady Javotte," for that was the name of the elder sister, "will you please loan me your yellow dress which you wear every day, that I may go?"

At this Lady Javotte laughed and said that she would never think of loaning her dress to a cinder-maid. Cinderella was very glad indeed to hear this because she really would not have known what to do if Lady Javotte had been willing to loan her the dress.

The next evening, after the sisters had gone to the ball, the fairy godmother appeared. Touching Cinderella again with her wand, she made her even more beautiful than the night before. As Cinderella drove away, the fairy godmother warned her to leave the ball before midnight.

The Prince was waiting for her when she reached the Palace. He led her once more to the place of honor and never left her all during the evening. Cinderella enjoyed herself so much that the time slipped by unnoticed. Just as supper was being served the clock began to strike the hour of twelve. She suddenly remembered the fairy's warning. Rising to her feet she ran swiftly out of the Palace. In her haste, she dropped one of her crystal slippers on the steps. The Prince who was following

her quickly picked it up and slipped it into his pocket. Looking up, he saw that the Princess had disappeared.

When Cinderella reached home all she had left of her lovely clothes was one little crystal slipper; the Prince had the mate to it.

The Prince asked the guards if they had seen the Princess, but they had seen only a little beggar maiden, dressed in rags, slipping through the Palace Gates.

Cinderella waited for the sisters to come home, and asked them if the Princess had been at the ball.

"Yes," said they, "and she was even more beautiful than the evening before. But suddenly, at twelve o'clock she disappeared, and no one knew where she had gone." They told her, however, that the Prince had found one of her crystal slippers. She had dropped it in her flight and they were certain that he would find her no matter where she was hidden.

The Prince asked everyone if they knew anything about the Princess, but no one was able to help him.

At last he sent out messengers with trumpets announcing to all that he would marry whomever the slipper would fit. This caused great excitement in the

kingdom. Every lady hoped that the crystal slipper would fit her.

First the slipper was tried on all the princesses, then on all the duchesses, then on all the grand ladies, and at last it came to the home of the two sisters. Each, of course, tried to force her foot into it, but the little slipper would not fit either of them.

Cinderella, who was standing watching, at last asked, timidly, "May I try?"

At this the sisters laughed and cried, "What! a cinder-maid try on the crystal slipper?"

The messenger looked at Cinderella and thought her very fair indeed, and replied, "The Prince said that every maiden in the kingdom, could, if she wished, try on the slipper."

Cinderella then seated herself on a stool. The messenger knelt before her and put the slipper on her foot. It fitted her as if it had been made for her, and so it had. Then, to the great amazement of the sisters, Cinderella drew the other slipper out of her pocket and slipped it on her foot.

At that moment her fairy godmother appeared. Touching Cinderella with her wand, she changed her once more into the beautiful Princess.

When the sisters saw that Cinderella was the lovely lady of the ball, they knelt before her, begging her forgiveness. She put her arms around them, raised them to their feet, and told them that she forgave them freely.

The messenger then led Cinderella to the Palace

LOIS LENSKI

where the Prince was waiting for her. In a few days they were married in royal state and lived happily ever after.